Balletball

Erin Dionne • Illustrated by Gillian Flint

ｉ⌒ｉ Charlesbridge

For Roxy—E. D.

For Jen and Senna—G. F.

Published by Charlesbridge
85 Main Street, Watertown, MA 02472
(617) 926-0329 • www.charlesbridge.com

Library of Congress Cataloging-in-Publication Data
Names: Dionne, Erin, 1975– author. | Flint, Gillian, illustrator.
Title: Balletball / Erin Dionne; illustrated by Gillian Flint.
Description: Watertown, MA: Charlesbridge, [2020] |
Summary: Nini loves ballet, not sports, so when her mother signs her up to
    play baseball she sulks until the coach explains how baseball and ballet
    can go together—and when a timely plié in the outfield saves the game
    she realizes that "balletball" is really not so bad after all.
Identifiers: LCCN 2018058507 (print) | LCCN 2019000672 (ebook) |
    ISBN 9781632897978 (ebook) | ISBN 9781632897985 (ebook pdf) |
    ISBN 9781580899390 (reinforced for library use)
Subjects: LCSH: Baseball stories. | Ballet—Juvenile fiction. |
    Motivation (Psychology)—Juvenile fiction. | CYAC: Baseball—Fiction. |
    Ballet—Fiction. | Motivation (Psychology)—Fiction.
Classification: LCC PZ7.D6216 (ebook) | LCC PZ7.D6216 Bal 2020 (print) |
    DDC   [E]—dc23
LC record available at https://lccn.loc.gov/2018058507

Printed in China
(hc) 10 9 8 7 6 5 4 3 2 1

Illustrations done in watercolor and brushpen on 100% cotton
    hot-pressed watercolor paper
Display type set in Sant Elia Script Alt by Ryan Martinson of Yellow Design Studio
Text type set in ITC Bookman by Adobe
Printed by 1010 Printing International Limited in Huizhou, Guangdong, China
Production supervision by Brian G. Walker
Designed by Sarah Richards Taylor

Nini loved dancing ballet.
She loved to leap.
And twirl. And plié.
And she really loved her sparkly tutu.

The week after her recital,
Nini raced for her ballet shoes.

"Not today," said her mom. "Today you have baseball practice!"

"Baseball?" asked Nini.

"Baseball," repeated her mother. "Remember? We signed up during the winter."

Nini did not remember.

She trudged to her room. She wanted to dance.

"You cannot wear your tutu to baseball practice," her mother said.

Nini frowned and changed her clothes.
She decided right then that she did
not like baseball.

At the park Coach handed her a lumpy brown glove and sent her to the uneven, grassy field.

Nini looked at the glove
and whispered,

"You are ugly."

She missed her pink ballet
shoes and the smooth, shiny
studio floor.

"There is no leaping in baseball!"
Coach called.

And then, "There is no twirling
in baseball!"

And eventually, "There is no flopping in baseball!"

And later, "Nini! There are no ballet moves in baseball!"

It's a plié, thought Nini.

Not even when she took her turn at bat, and Coach showed her how to swing and run if she hit the ball—not even then did Nini like baseball.

(Though she did like the running part.
A little.)

"I want my tutu! And my sparkles!" she wailed to her mother. "I want to leap and twirl and plié."

"But there is no ballet right now,"
her mother explained. "There's baseball.
You signed up for baseball."

Nini scowled.

At practice she did not want to stand in the outfield. She did not want to wear her yellow-and-blue uniform. She did not want to keep her eye on the ball.

Her teammates frowned. "Ballet girl," they said, "you have to follow the rules."

"Baseball is about working together," Coach told the team. He looked right at Nini. "Just like in a show, everyone does their part."

Nini scowled again.

At the team's first game, Nini trudged
to the outfield. She watched the clouds,
not the ball.

She counted the stitches on her glove.
She spun like a helicopter at her turn at bat.

And she frowned when her teammates told her she had not done her part.

Before the next game,
Coach called the whole team
to a meeting.

"Winning isn't everything,"
he said. "It's trying your best
that's most important."

Everyone looked at Nini.
She made a fierce face.
She headed even more slowly
than usual toward the field.
Coach asked her to wait.

"I don't like baseball. I like to dance,"
Nini said before Coach could say anything.

"Did you know," he said, "that some
professional athletes take ballet?"

Nini, who did not want to listen,
paid attention.

"They use it to be faster and more agile. Baseball and ballet can go together," Coach said.
On the field she tried. A little.

Coach took Nini aside again the next week.

"Baseball can sparkle," he said. He handed her shoelaces that glittered blue and yellow in the sun.

"It's too bad these have to go on baseball shoes," she said. But she grinned at him when she laced them up.

Nini crossed her arms in the outfield.
But she watched the batter. And the ball.
 Her team scored three runs. The other
team scored one. And another.
 Nini was worried. What if her team
lost again?

The game was almost over.

The biggest kid on the other team was up at bat. He swung. The ball went *crack!* off the bat. It flew through the air . . .

straight at Nini.

The roar of the crowd rose through the park like waves. The ball was going to fall behind her.

Nini leaped.

She twirled.

She tried.

And as the ball came down,
she pliéd.

The hard round baseball
landed right . . .

. . . in her glove.

The cheers from the crowd were
just as loud as the applause from
the audience at her recital.
Nini's team won!

Nini tossed the ball to her teammate.
She ran to the bench to give high fives
to the other team.

"Great job, Nini!" Coach called.
"What was that?"
She curtsied. She smiled.
"Balletball," she said.